1976 - '77

Little Bat's Secret

Little Bat's Secret

By Kathy Darling

Drawings by Cyndy Szekeres

GARRARD PUBLISHING COMPANY
CHAMPAIGN, ILLINOIS

Little Bat's Secret

The wind blew a cloud
across the yellow moon.
It rattled the windows
of the old house
on the hill.
Down the crooked chimney
it howled.
Woo-oo-oo. Woo-oo-oo.

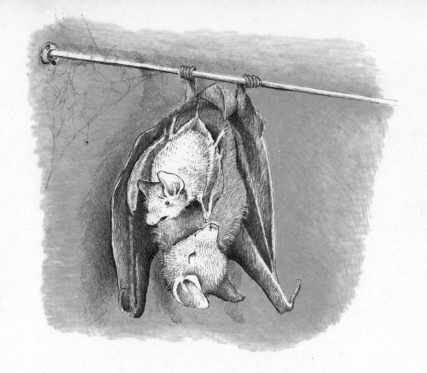

"What was that?"
asked Little Bat.
The cold wind
danced across her fur.
Woo-oo-oo. Woo-oo-oo.
The spooky noise grew louder.
"Mother, I'm scared,"
called Little Bat.

Mother Bat yawned
and stretched her wings.
"It's only the night wind,"
she said.
"It is telling us
to wake up."

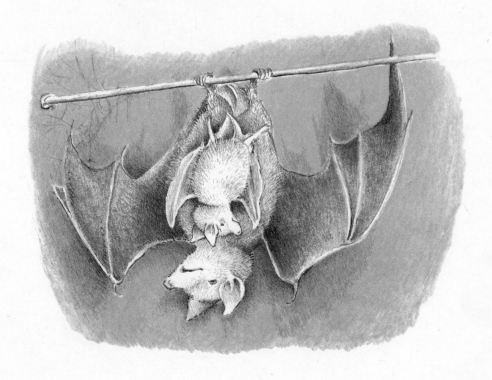

Before very long
all the brown bats
in the old house
heard the night wind.
They stretched
and squeaked.

Carefully,
they washed their fur.
Then, like a puff of brown smoke,
they rushed up the chimney
and flew out
into the night.

"Come on, Little Bat,"
said mother.
"It's time for us to go, too."
"I'm afraid of the dark,"
squeaked Little Bat.
"Will you carry me, mother?"
she asked.
"You are old enough
to fly by yourself,"
she answered.
"I might fall," cried Little Bat.
"Flap your wings
before you let go,"
said mother.
Little Bat flapped one wing.
Then she tried the other one.
She was flying!

"Follow me
up the crooked chimney,"
said mother.
Little Bat squeaked loudly.
She didn't want to go.
But she was afraid
to stay alone in the house.
So up the chimney she flew.
"You are flying very well,"
said mother.
"Stick out your tail.
Then you can do tricks."
Little Bat did a somersault.
Then she flew loops
around the chimney.
Just for fun she played tag
with a moonbeam.

"Now we must go
and find dinner,"
said Mother Bat.
"Watch me, little one.
I will teach you
how to catch bugs."

Zip—she caught a big fat fly.

Zap—she grabbed a shiny beetle.

Zoom—she gobbled up an orange moth.

"The pond is a good place
to get food,"
said mother.
"I want to find
a mosquito for dinner."
"Wait,
please wait for me,"
squeaked Little Bat.

"Don't fly so fast,
mother," she called.
"I can't keep up."
Mother Bat disappeared
into the black night.
Little Bat was alone.
"Come back," she squealed.
"Don't leave me, mother."

Where, oh, where had mother gone?

Little Bat looked everywhere.

She could not see mother.

She could not see the old house.

She was lost.

In the branches of a big oak tree,

she saw a dark shape.

"Mother," she cried

with a happy squeak.

Suddenly, the dark shape

turned two big, yellow eyes

on Little Bat.

"SCREECH!"

It was an owl.

His claws were sharp.

His wings were strong,

and he was hungry!

Little Bat

was afraid for her life.

She flew quickly away.

Her wings hurt

and her heart thumped.

She was tired,

too tired to flap her wings

against a big puff of wind.

Down, down she fell
with a splash into the pond.
The water made little circles
in the moonlight
as Little Bat swam.
Her tiny wings paddled
through the dark water.

Deep in the pond
a big fish watched.
He moved
toward the swimming bat
like a silver flash.

But he was too late.
Little Bat crawled
out onto the grass
just ahead
of his open mouth.

The pond
was a dangerous place
for little bats.
So was the grass.
A big, black snake
came creepy, creep.

"Mother," yelled Little Bat.
She crawled
through the grass
as fast as she could.
The snake followed her
up a tree.
But when she was high enough,
Little Bat flew away.

She came to rest
in an old, dead tree.
Hanging upside down,
Little Bat dried her fur.
She cried for her mother.
Then she heard a noise.
It was a very little noise.
The noise came again.
"Help! Help!"
"Who is it?"
called Little Bat.
"What is the matter?"
"I'm trapped,"
answered the voice.
"The monster is coming.
He will eat me up.
Please help me!"

"I can't see," said Little Bat.
"It's too dark."
All at once a light flashed on.
There,
caught in a spider's web,
was a firefly.
His light flashed on and off.
A spider was moving toward him
on eight hairy legs.
Little Bat flew toward the spider
and squeaked loudly.
She frightened
the hairy monster away.
Then Little Bat broke the web
with her teeth.
She helped the firefly
out of the trap.

"Thank you, thank you,"
said the firefly
as he cleaned
the last bits of web
from his wings.
"You saved my life."

Little Bat began to cry.
"Would you please
turn your light back on?"
she squeaked.
"I'm afraid of the dark.
I'm cold
and I'm lost too."

"Why don't you
put *your* light on?"
asked the firefly.
"I don't have one,"
cried Little Bat.
"Don't be afraid,"
said the firefly.
"I will be your light.

You helped me.
Now I will help you."
The firefly lit up.
Then he climbed up
on Little Bat's head.
"Let's look
over this way,"
he said.

"Mother," called Little Bat.
"Where are you?"
She swooped and zoomed
across the night sky.
But mother did not answer.
In a flash of firefly light,
they saw a bat.
"Look, Little Bat,
there is your mother,"
said the firefly.
They followed the big bat.
"Wait, mother, wait for me,"
called Little Bat.
The big bat did not hear her.
It flew like a moving shadow
into a hole.
It was a great cave.

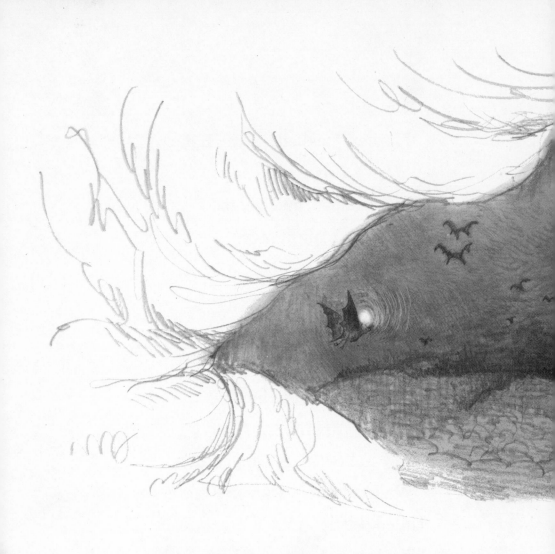

Inside the cave were more bats.

There were hundreds of bats.

There were thousands of bats.

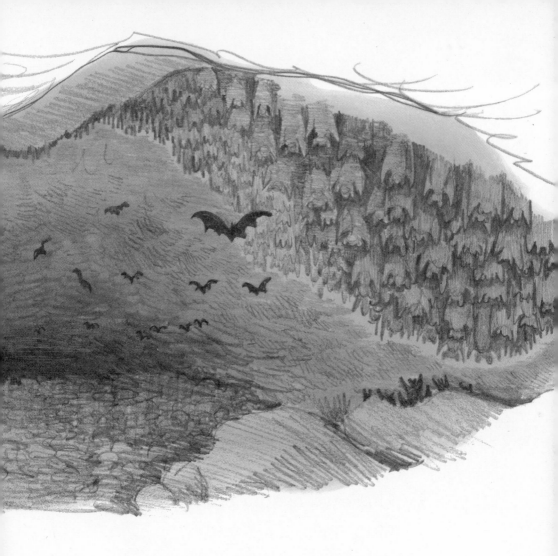

But these bats were not brown
like Little Bat.
They were gray.

They pushed and shoved
to get the best spots
on the cave walls.
Their squeaks filled the cave.
Little Bat yelled "mother"
as loud as she could.
She could not be heard
over the noisy gray bats.
More and more bats
flew into the cave.
They were gray too.
This cave had no brown bats.
Little Bat soon found
that her mother
was not there.
Sadly, she flew out
of the cave.

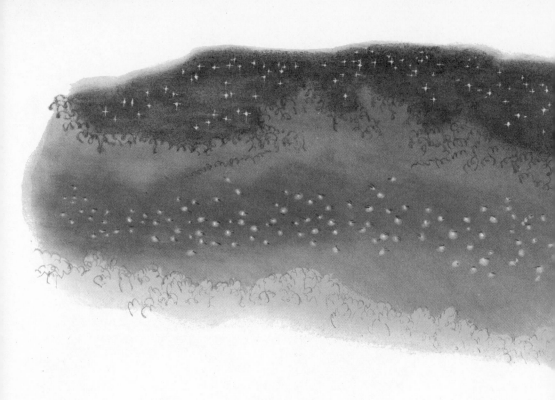

"What can we do, firefly?"
asked Little Bat.
"How will I ever get home?"
The bat and the firefly
heard a cricket call.
The wind became still.
The clouds drifted away.

Above them the sky
was filled with twinkling lights.
Below them
light twinkled back.
It was firefly meadow.

Firefly blinked a signal
to his friends.
They flew up
to meet him.

"This is my friend
Little Bat," he said.
"She saved me
from the spider.

Little Bat is lost,"
said the firefly.
"She lives in the old house
on the hill.
Does anyone know
how to get there?"
"I do,"
said the biggest firefly.
"Fly straight past
those three pine trees.
Then look for a rock
shaped like a turtle.
Turn left.
Then you will see your home."
"I must leave you now,"
said the firefly.
"Fly home safely, Little Bat."

Little Bat folded her wing
around the firefly
and hugged him.
"Friend," she said,
"I will be back
tomorrow night."

The stars twinkled brightly.
Little Bat flew off
toward the three pine trees.

The night wind blew.
The dark clouds
covered the moon.
Little Bat could not see.
"Maybe I won't find
turtle rock," she worried.

She looked and looked
as she flew
close to the ground.
She saw something
that looked like a house.

With a zig and a zag,
Little Bat
flew closer to it.

Little Bat
flew right into a barn.
She knew she was not home.
There were no bats here.
She was very afraid.

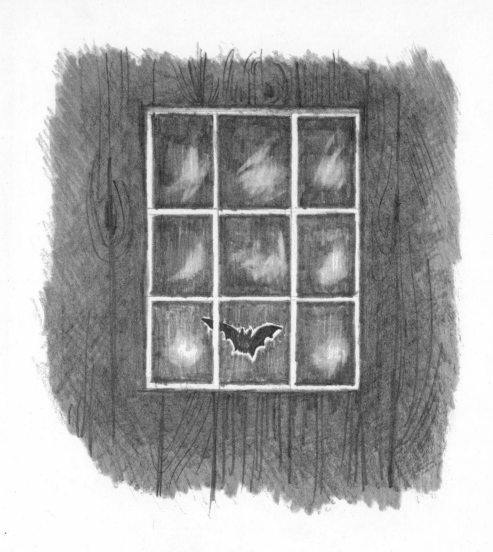

Little Bat
flew around wildly,
trying to get out.

She hit a plow.

She ran into the cow.

She flew through a haystack.

"SQUEAK!"
cried Little Bat.
She was tangled
in a rope.
Each time she hit something
she squeaked again.

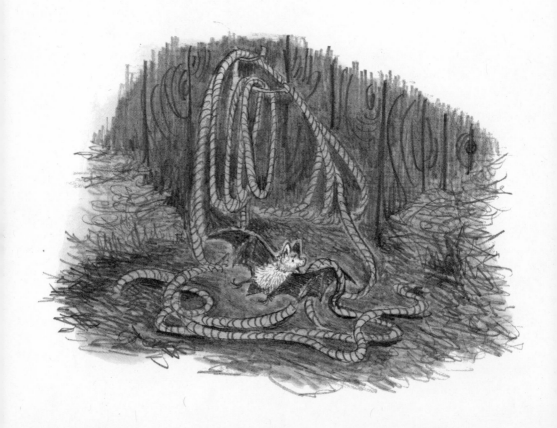

A barn swallow
watched Little Bat
from high up.
Louder and louder
the baby bat cried.
Back and forth
bounced the squeaky noises.

"Little Bat,"
called the barn swallow.
"I will tell you a secret.
You have a special power.
Listen to your squeaks.
Then you will be able
to fly safely in the dark."
Little Bat
listened to her squeaks.
She began to fly around things
instead of into them.
Soon she could fly
around the barn at full speed.
"Whee," cried Little Bat.
"I don't need
a night light.
I have squeak power.

Thank you, swallow,"
called Little Bat.
She flew out of the barn.
"I can have fun
in the dark now."

The special power
worked outside too.
Little Bat closed her eyes.
She found that she could
bounce her voice
off trees and rocks.
It was easy to fly
in the dark now.

She was having so much fun
she didn't see the rock
shaped like a turtle.
But she did see the old house.
Inside she found mother.

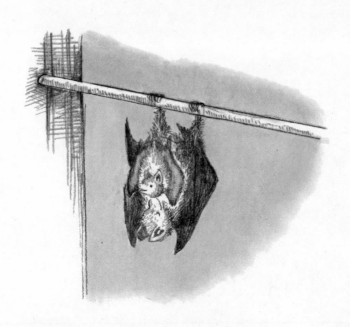

"Where have you been?"
asked mother.
"I was starting out
to look for you."
"I learned the secret,"
said Little Bat.
Mother didn't answer.
She was already asleep.

Little Bat
snuggled into her mother's
warm fur.
"I can't wait
to tell firefly
about my special power,"
she thought.
"I can't wait until tomorrow."